People of the Bible

The Bible through stories and pictures

Ruth's Story

Presented to

SANDRA MAC KENZIE

GLENURQUHART FREE

CHURCH SUNDAY SCHOOL

JUNE 88.

Ruth's Story

Retold by Catherine Storr
Pictures by Geoff Taylor

Methuen Children's Books
in association with Belitha Press Ltd

One year when there was a famine in Judea,
a man called Elimelech
travelled to the land of Moab to find food.
He brought with him his wife, Naomi,
and his two sons.
After a time, Elimelech died and left Naomi a widow.
Her sons married two Moabite girls, Ruth and Orpah.
They all lived in that land for ten years.

Then both the sons died.
Naomi decided to go back to Bethlehem
in Judea, her own country, for the famine was over.
She said to Ruth and Orpah,
'I am going back to Judea. You two should stay here,
and find yourselves husbands to look after you.
The men of Judea will never marry Moabite girls.'
Both the girls wept. They said,
'No, we will go with you.'
Naomi said, 'You had better stay here.
I shall never find another husband.
Even if I did, and had more sons,
they would be too young for you to marry.'

Orpah agreed that she would stay in Moab.
But Ruth said, 'Don't ask me to leave you.
Where you go, I will go.
Where you stay, I will stay.
Your people shall be my people,
and your God shall be my God.
Where you die, I will die and there I will be buried.
Only death shall part us.'
Naomi saw that Ruth meant what she said.
So they travelled together back to Bethlehem.

They arrived in Bethlehem
at the beginning of the barley harvest.
Ruth said to Naomi,
'Let me go to glean in the fields.'
She meant to pick up the ears of corn
left by the young men as they reaped the harvest.
Naomi said, 'Yes, go, my daughter.'
It happened by chance
that the field Ruth went to belonged to Boaz,
a rich man, and a cousin of Naomi's husband.

Boaz saw Ruth gleaning in his field.
He asked who she was. The head reaper said,
'That is Ruth, the Moabitess,
who has come here with Naomi, her mother-in-law.'

Boaz said to Ruth, 'Don't go to any other fields.
I have told my young men not to worry you.
If you are thirsty,
you can drink from the pitchers of water
which the reapers have drawn from the well.'

Ruth bowed low before Boaz, and she said,
'Why are you so kind to me? I am a stranger.'
Boaz said, 'I know
that you have left your own country
and your mother and father
to come here to Bethlehem with Naomi.
The Lord will take care of you and bless you.'

Ruth thanked him and said,
'Look on me kindly, my lord.
You have comforted me
and spoken to me in friendship,
as if I were one of your handmaidens.'

Boaz said to Ruth,
'When you are hungry, come and sit with the reapers
and eat with them.'
After Ruth had eaten and left,
Boaz told his reapers to allow her to glean
and sometimes to let some handfuls of barley grain
fall where she would find them.
That evening Ruth took home
a large measure of barley grain.
She also gave Naomi food
which she had saved from the reapers' meal.

Naomi asked Ruth, 'Where did you glean today?
Who has given you all this?'
Ruth said,
'The man whose field I was in is called Boaz.'
Naomi said, 'God is being very kind to us.
Boaz is a cousin of ours,
one of the closest relations we have.
Don't go and glean in a field
belonging to anyone else.'

At the end of the harvest,
Naomi said to Ruth,
'Every night, Boaz goes to the threshing floor
to winnow his corn.
Put on your best clothes and go there this evening.
Don't let him see you until he has eaten and drunk.

Then go and uncover his feet,
and he will tell you what to do.'
That evening, Ruth went to the threshing floor,
and waited till Boaz had eaten and drunk.
When he laid himself down to sleep,
Ruth laid herself down at his feet.

At midnight, Boaz woke and saw Ruth lying at his feet.
He said, 'Who are you?'
Ruth answered, 'I am Ruth.
I am your servant, and a cousin of yours.'
Boaz said, 'The Lord bless you, my daughter.
I will do everything you ask.
But there is one man
who is a closer cousin of yours than I am.
He should look after you and Naomi.'
In the morning, Boaz filled Ruth's veil with barley
for her to take home.

The next day,
Boaz went to the gate of the city
and waited until he saw the man
who was Naomi's and Ruth's closest cousin.
He said to the man,
'Naomi, your kinswoman,
has come back to the city.
She has a piece of land to sell.
Because you are nearest to her in kin,
you have the first right to buy it if you want to.'
The man said, 'Yes, I will buy it.'

Boaz said, 'The land also belongs to Ruth, the Moabitess.
If you take the land, you must also look after her.'
Then the man said, 'No, I can't afford to do that.
You are the next cousin in line.
You can buy the land instead of me.'
When he said this, the man took off his shoe,
for this was the custom in Israel,
when a bargain was struck.

Then Boaz said to the elders of the people,
'You are witnesses that I have bought the land,
and I have also taken Ruth for my wife.'
The elders said,
'We are witnesses of what you are doing.
The Lord bless you.'

Some time after Ruth and Boaz were married,
Ruth had a baby son.
The people said to Naomi,
'The Lord has blessed you.
Here is a grandson
to look after you in your old age.'

Then Naomi was glad.
She took the baby and cared for it.
He was called Obed, the servant of God.
He became the father of Jesse,
whose son, David, was made King of all Israel.

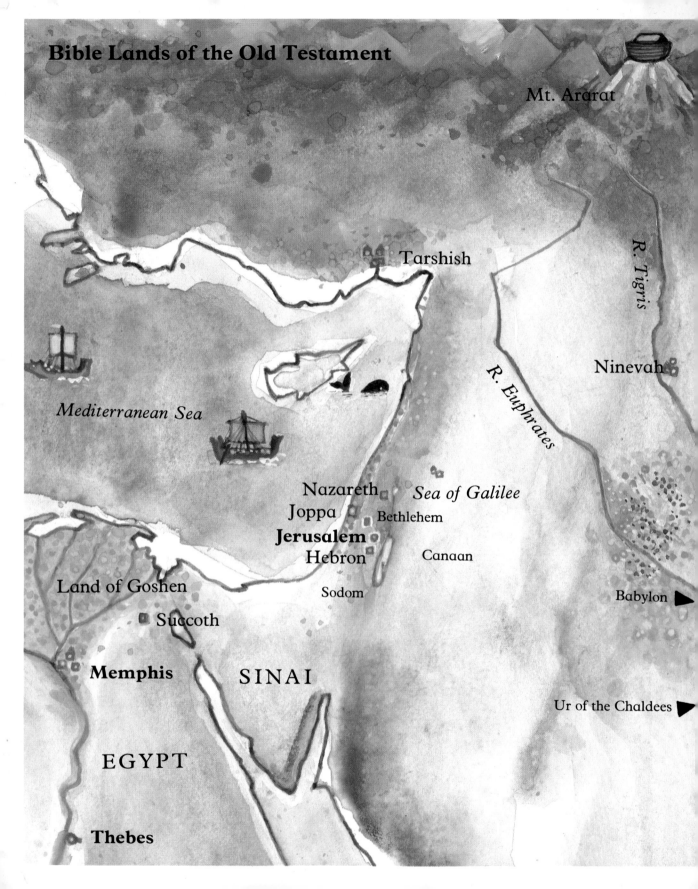